Little Puppy
and the
Big
Green
Monster

To Conrad!

by Mike Wohnoutka

Mike W...
April # 2017

Holiday House / New York

To Anna, Franklin, and Olivia

With special thanks to my editor, Grace Maccarone, and my writers' group:
John Coy, David LaRochelle, Janet Lawson, Jody Peterson Lodge, and Cindy Rogers.
Without all your insight and encouragement, this book would not have been possible.

Copyright © 2014 by Mike Wohnoutka
All Rights Reserved
HOLIDAY HOUSE is registered in the U.S. Patent and Trademark Office.
Printed and Bound in April 2014 at Toppan Leefung, DongGuan City, China.
The artwork was created with acrylic paint.
www.holidayhouse.com
First Edition
1 3 5 7 9 10 8 6 4 2

Library of Congress Cataloging-in-Publication Data
Wohnoutka, Mike, author, illustrator.
Little puppy and the big green monster / by Mike Wohnoutka. — First edition.
pages cm
Summary: A puppy invites a monster to play with him, but soon discovers that the monster is not very good
at such games as tag or hide-and-seek.
ISBN 978-0-8234-3064-2 (hardcover)
[1. Play—Fiction. 2. Dogs—Fiction. 3. Animals—Infancy—Fiction. 4. Monsters—Fiction.] I. Title.
PZ7.W81813Lit 2014
[E]—dc23
2013037252

Who wants to play?

Too busy.

Arf
Arf

Too lazy.

Arf
Arf

Too mean!

Too boring.

There's no one to play with.

He will play with me.

Let's play!

Arf
Arf

ROAR!

Do you like
to play ball?

ROAR!

How about a game
of catch?

I'll get it.

Got it!

Now let's play hide-and-seek.

He's not very
good at this.

Tag! You're it!

Where are
you going?

Oh, you want to race!

SLAM!

Hide-and-seek again?

Now I'm it!

Found you!

slip

Splash!

cough
cough

lick

click

MIKE WOHNOUTKA has illustrated many books for children, including *Jack's House*, written by Karen Magnuson Beil and honored as a Bank Street College of Education Best Children's Book, and *Hanukkah Bear*, written by Eric A. Kimmel and praised in a starred review from *School Library Journal* as "successful on every level." *Little Puppy and the Big Green Monster* is his first book as author and illustrator. His website is www.mikewohnoutka.com.